My Lamb Finds

The Castle Library with the Clock Tower

31:05:2019

DEAR TIA

ALL MY LOVE

LAMMY

X X X

WRITTEN BY
CHRISTINE BOWEN

ILLUSTRATED BY
A.J.BOWEN

GRAPHICS BY
DANIEL T. ADAMS

ISBN: 1721780645
ISBN-13: 978-1721780648

Book design and layout by:
One Spark Media
www.onesparkmedia.com
For more information about the author and this Children's Book, visit:
www.christinebowen.org

Dedicated to those who hear the bells of life and make the journey to discover what they mean. Time is yours.

For Joey, Jack, Gabriel, and Michael.

My Lamb was walking along the meadow path when suddenly it started to rain. He stood under a grand maple tree to keep dry. There, a large eagle swooped down and sat on a low branch.

The eagle called down, "Hello there. My name is Mr. Eagle. How are you today, little lamb?"
My Lamb answered, "I am fine, Mr. Eagle. My name is My Lamb. I'm trying to stay dry from all this rain."

Mr. Eagle said, "Indeed, My Lamb. However, the wildflowers will be happy with this rain." "You appear to be in a hurry, Mr. Eagle," My Lamb observed as Mr. Eagle looked for a clearing in the sky.

"I am short on time, My Lamb. You see, I am journeying to the Clock Tower," said Mr. Eagle. "What is a Clock Tower?" My Lamb asked. Mr. Eagle smiled. "A Clock Tower is where you will find your purpose in time. Time is flying."

"Can I come? I want to find my purpose in time also," My Lamb pleaded. "Time is short. I cannot wait for you, My Lamb. I must go now," Mr. Eagle said.

"Can you please tell me where the Clock Tower is so that I may journey there too?" My Lamb asked.

Mr. Eagle pronounced, "The Clock Tower is in the Castle Library. You must travel to the far side of the meadow and go through the forest of evergreens. There you will find a small town where white flowering pear trees line the streets."

"The Clock Tower can be seen, and you can hear its bells, from anywhere in the town. Look for the tallest building. Follow the sound of its bells," Mr. Eagle said as he flew away.

My Lamb eagerly left to search for the forest of evergreens. When he saw the tall green trees, he ran as fast as he could through them until he found the small town.

My Lamb saw the flowering pear trees lining the steets and sidewalks. He spotted a big tall castle that loomed towards the sky. He had found the Castle Library that Mr. Eagle had told him about.

There was a large fountain in front of the Castle Library. Thirsty, My Lamb drank the cool water and was refreshed.

My Lamb walked up the steps of the Castle Library and through the open doors. He admired the old, wooden plank floors that stretched from the front door to the back of the library.

On the front desk were freshly-baked oatmeal raisin cookies. My Lamb enjoyed one.
The Castle Library had many rooms filled with interesting books about animals, oceans, sailing, people from far-away lands, storybooks, and much more.

My Lamb began to flip through a colorful book when he heard a pitter-patter from the floor above. Curious, he made his way to the back of the Castle Library where the staircase was located.

At the top of the stairs, My Lamb discovered a bronze plaque which stated that the courthouse was built in the year 1891. "Wowzers!" said My Lamb. "The Castle Library was once a courthouse that changed over time."

My Lamb entered through the door at the top of the stairs. On the back wall, there were four handmade tapestries that told the history of a small town and the love of a community.

An image of a mighty eagle, soaring majestically, much like Mr. Eagle, was woven into the timeless story in each of the tapestries.

"Shazam!" exclaimed My Lamb as he gazed upon four huge stained glass windows. "Look how the beautiful light from the windows spill color onto this old wood floor."

Beneath the haze of the stained glass light, My Lamb saw a little girl with golden curls, big blue eyes, and rosy cheeks. She was dressed in a yellow tutu with pink ballet shoes.

With her arms arched over her head, she was dancing on the purple squares that spilled to the floor from the sun streaming through the stained glass panes of the windows.

"Hello. My name is My Lamb. I'm looking for the Clock Tower." The little girl looked up and smiled.

"Hi, I'm Hope and I love to dance in the rays of the purple lights. They always show up at this time of the day, just before the clock tower bells ring."

Leaping from purple light to purple light, Hope said, "You can find the Clock Tower through the double doors at the rear of the courtroom. Explore the room and see what you can find. After all, it's all about time."

My Lamb laughed. "Yes it is. Thank you, Hope."

My Lamb continued to explore and saw two brick fireplaces on either side of the grand, wooden judge's bench. He also saw worn bookcases filled with old dusty books. He headed towards the double doors that led to the Clock Tower.

Hope hollered, "The clock bells are ready to ring anytime now. I love to dance to their song." My Lamb smiled as he nudged open the double doors to find a small museum of timeless courthouse memories.

Encased in glass was an old, Navy uniform with a picture of the sailor who had worn it, and the story of the war he fought many years ago.

My Lamb saw an old, faded lacey hat. It belonged to the wife of a soldier who fought in another war at another time. My Lamb felt as if he was a part of their story in history.

My Lamb could picture how life was in the past as he heard time ticking away. Tick. Tock. Tick. Tock.

To the right was a single door with a half glass pane. My Lamb saw the large clock inside. "I found the Clock Tower!" he hollered out to Hope.

My Lamb watched the large, brass pendulum swing as the clock ticked away. Suddenly the bells began to ring. The music filled up My Lamb's heart with joy.

The Clock Tower revealed to
My Lamb that time makes
history. He could hear the
memories of the past singing
out through the bells that
rang throughout the town,
through the tapestries that
hung on the wall, and
through the lights that spilled
onto the wood floor.

From the window, My Lamb saw Mr. Eagle flying by in peaceful harmony. He was dancing on a breeze with the flowering pear trees. Curious, My Lamb ran back into the courthouse, anxious to ask Hope why the Clock Tower was there.

Hope giggled. "The Clock Tower rings in song for the many people who pass through this courthouse. Time flies, My Lamb, and you can't hold onto it. Time is a special gift."

Hope pointed to the American Flag and said, "This courthouse sings a song of freedom and justice. Like the Pledge of Allegiance says, 'one nation, under God, indivisible, with liberty and justice for all.' That's what it's all about."

Hope smiled. "My Lamb, make your time as fragrant and full as the blossoming flowers of the pear tree. Make your time soar high, as an eagle in flight."

"Dance through the patterns that the sunlight colors on the ground wherever you stand. Let your song resound through time, as the Clock Tower bell sings to everyone and everything."

My Lamb danced alongside Hope until the purple pattern of the lights began to fade away, as did the time of day. As the sun was setting, My Lamb and Hope walked outside and gazed up at the Clock Tower, rejoicing in the memories and the ringing bells once more.

My Lamb knew that his life was his dance, and that the sun would color the purple patterns for him to dance upon. He learned that his time on earth could impact history. He had a purpose. His time was now.

Time is a journey that begins with your first breath. Live your time. Love your life.

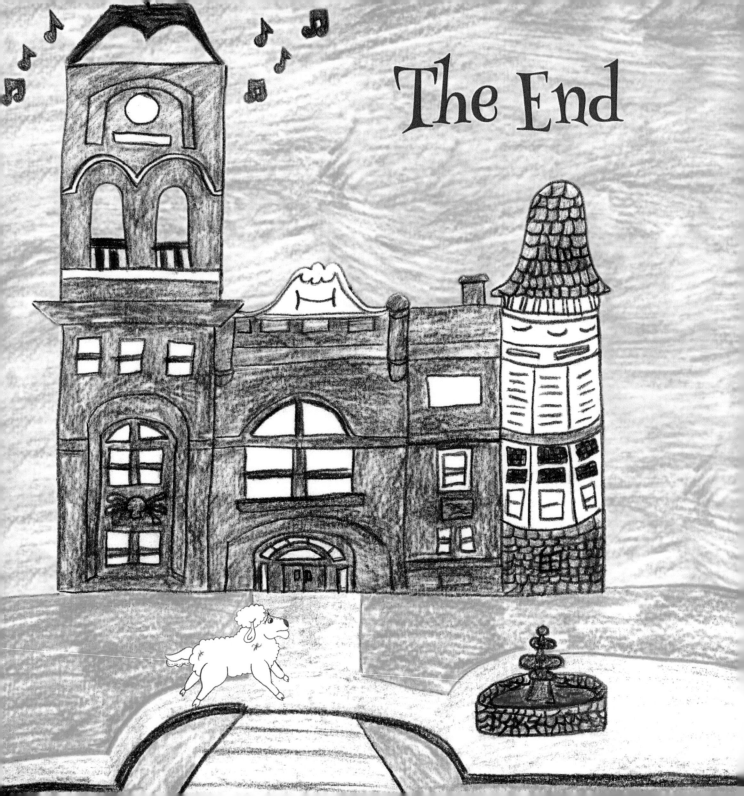

Don't forget to get your copies of Books 1 and 2 of the "My Lamb" series:

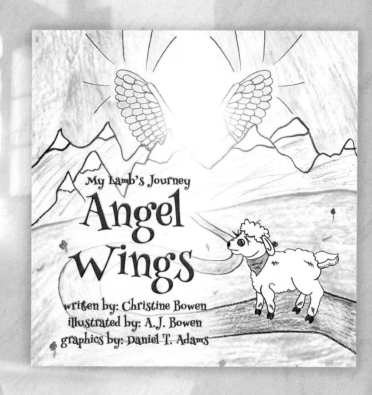

For more information about the author, and other books available, please visit the Official Christine Bowen website at www.christinebowen.org.

Buchanan, Georgia

Thank you to Buchanan-Haralson Public Library (The Castle Library), and Librarian Jana Gentry, in Buchanan, Georgia, for inspiring me with this wonderful true story of the little girl who danced in the light that fell from the stained glass windows in the courthouse.

The courthouse, the tapestries, the museum, the library, and the Clock Tower breathe the stories of a time long past. The Castle Library is an example of true small town American spirit. It was an honor spending time there. I will never forget taking a step back in time at the Castle Library and the Clock Tower. I will always be thankful for the wonderful hospitality of a very historical town.

My Lamb Finds Time: The Castle Library with the Clock Tower
Book Three of the "My Lamb" Series

www.christinebowen.org

A
ONE SPARK MEDIA
PUBLICATION

www.onesparkmedia.com

The "My Lamb" character is based on the True Witness band logo.

Heather Adams, of the award-winning rock band True Witness, created a hand-made, "My Lamb" stuffed animal which is what inspired the concept for the "My Lamb" book series. Heather hand-stitches every "My Lamb" toy. She treasures each lamb while designing them to be unique unto themselves. Special thanks to Heather Adams for pouring her joy and light into the world.

"My Lamb" has made his way into the hearts of many children and adults alike. He puts a smile on the faces of all who open their hearts to receive him.

Like "My Lamb", we all were created to be different. We bear different scars in life, yet Love is the unifying power that helps us to overcome, have hope, and believe.

To order your very own "My Lamb" stuffed animal, please visit the True Witness website at www.truewitness.com. The lambs come in a variety of colors.

Stay tuned for the next book in the "My Lamb" book series.

www.truewitness.com

41257674R00030

Printed in Poland
by Amazon Fulfillment
Poland Sp. z o.o., Wrocław